# My Dog the Lawyer

## By Jeremy L. Hodge, DMD
## Illustrated by Alex Faverman

# Acknowledgements

To my beautiful wife, I am eternally grateful for all of your love and support, you give my life meaning. Thank you for all you do for me, thank you for believing in me.

I would like to thank my office manager and editor, Pam. Without her hard work, this book would still be stuck on my hard drive.

Thank you to my wonderful daughters, Mercedes, Avery, and Hailey. The Hailey in the book is really a composite of all three of my beautiful girls. You make my days brighter.

Finally, my little buddy Milo.

Created by Jeremy L. Hodge, DMD. Send correspondence to 9012 Mathis Ave, Manassas VA 20109. Illustrated by Alex Faverman; contact via criscoknight@gmail.com. Edited by Pam Mosbrucker.

Manufactured in the United States of America

10 9 8 7 6 5 4 3 2 1

ISBN-13: 978-1479145348
ISBN-10: 1479145343

Hi, I'm Hailey and I'm six years old. I have the best dog in the whole wide world.  His name is Milo.

A few nights ago I was in bed and I heard some strange noises outside my window. I ran to the window and outside I saw the craziest thing.

There were little tractors, trucks, and machines surrounding Milo's dog house. It was so loud!

I heard all kinds of noises, saws and hammers, and lots of talking. Milo was walking around and talking with another dog and they were both wearing hard hats.

I tried to open my window but my dad came into my room and told me to go back to bed.

He was really bossy and grumpy and I don't even know why.

I really don't like to be bossed. He said it was two in the morning and I needed to get back to sleep.

I climbed back into bed but I was so excited I couldn't sleep.

I kept wondering what all those tractors and machines were doing around Milo's dog house.

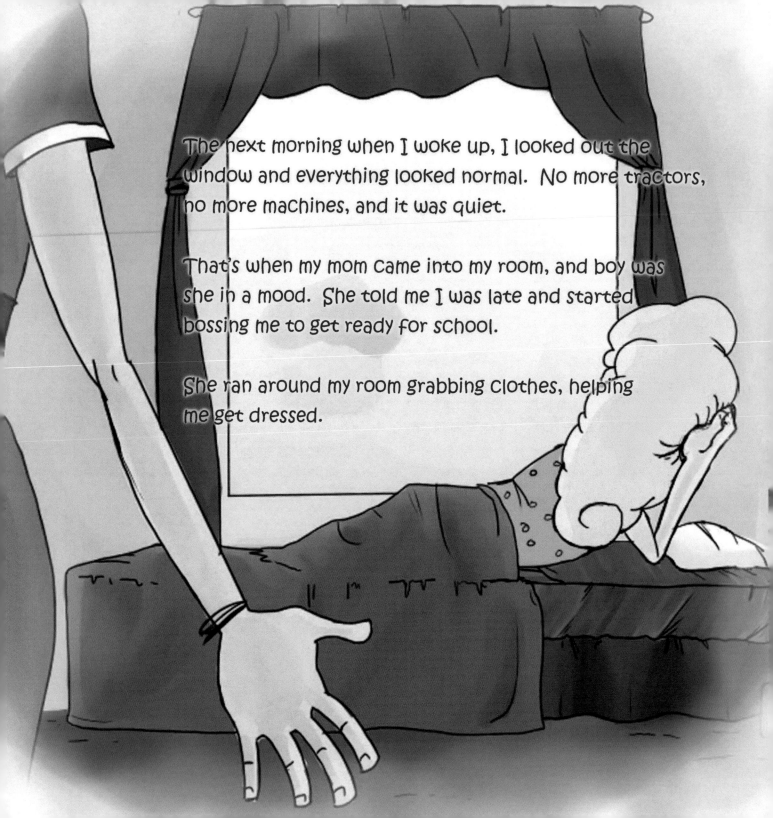

I had to eat a dumb old hard granola bar for breakfast because my mom said I slept in. She rushed me out the door and I started walking to school with my sisters.

I told them what I saw last night but they didn't believe me. They just kept saying that I was dreaming. My sisters just don't know anything important at all!

I tried to sit very still in class all day, but it was so hard. My teacher Miss Jones kept saying I was in trouble. I was just so excited to find out what happened last night that I couldn't sit still. When the bell finally rang, I ran all the way home. I didn't even wait for my sisters. I ran all around the house looking for Milo, but I couldn't find him anywhere.

He wasn't in my room, he wasn't in the kitchen begging for food, and he wasn't asleep in his bed. I even looked in our basement but he wasn't there either.

I ran back upstairs and my mom grabbed me and gave me a big squeeze. "How was your day?" she asked. I started to tell her all about what I saw last night. I told her about the tractors, and the loud noises, and Milo with his hard hat.

"That sounds very exciting, honey. You should hurry outside to see what was going on," she said. I'm sure she didn't really believe me, but I love my mom for trying to be mature.

I ran outside and looked at Milo's dog house.
It was just the same as always.

But then I peeked inside and couldn't believe what I saw. There was a huge room that looked like an office. A big bookshelf was on the wall and it was filled with really important-looking books.

On some of the walls were pictures of parks with lots of trees.

In the middle of the room was a small desk, and there was Milo typing on a computer. I couldn't believe it. My dog was typing, and he was wearing a shirt and tie. He looked so cute I wanted to squeeze him. I ran over to see what he was doing. "Milo, what's going on?" I asked.

"I'm working," he replied.

"Working! What are you working on, and where did you learn to type?" I asked.

"I learned how to type when I was in law school." Milo said.

"I didn't know you were a lawyer, my dad is a lawyer, when did you get to be a lawyer?" I asked.

"I went to Yardvard," he said. "Yardvard is the number one doggy law school in the country, and I graduated top in my class."

"I didn't know there was a doggy law school. That's so amazing! Hey, what was going on last night?"

"Schnikies! Did I wake you? I'm sorry," Milo said. "I used to have an office by the courthouse but I didn't like having to sneak away to get to work so I had my doghouse improved last night."

"Wow!" I said. "Tell me about law school, what kind of teachers did you have?"

"Well the dean of the school was a Great Dane, and the dog who taught us international law was a French Poodle, and her assistant was a Chihuahua," Milo said.

"We also had a Blood Hound named professor Schnoz, he was our ethics professor. Blood Hounds are great at teaching ethics because their noses are so good. They can easily sniff out what is right and wrong," said Milo.

"But we didn't just have dogs to teach us. We also had a Bald Eagle named Professor Stately who taught constitutional law. We had a rabbit named Professor Loper who taught us about family law. Rabbits usually like family law because they have such big families," Milo said.

"But my favorite professor was a Doberman Pinscher named Professor Gnarl. He was our trial law professor. Professor Gnarl helped me realize I wanted to become a trial lawyer," he said.

I couldn't believe it. My dog Milo was a lawyer. I told you he is awesome.

"What are you working on?" I asked.

"I am suing Balmart," Milo said. "They are discriminating against Afghan Hounds. They won't hire them because their hair is too long. Balmart also claims Afghan Hounds are unsanitary."

Milo smiled at me. "Balmart is wrong and I am going to prove it in court today."

Wow, my dog is really cool. He must be a great lawyer if he is taking on a company as big as Balmart.

"Wow Milo, I can't believe I never knew you were a lawyer. What other kinds of cases have you had?" I asked.

"This is the biggest case of my life. I have been working on it for months," he replied. "Before this I mostly handled dogs suing each other over toys or bones or sniffing each other."

"Wow, that is so neat! I'm so very proud of you." I said as I reached down and gave him a good scratch behind the ear.

"Schnikies!" Milo said as he looked at his watch. "I have to go to my case now it starts in one hour and I don't want to be late."

"Can I come along and watch? I really want to see what happens in doggy court."

"Sure," Milo said. "I would love to have you come along."

I was so excited to go to doggy court. I ran back inside and told my mom that I was going to court with Milo. She just laughed and told me to stay close to the house. I told you she didn't believe me. I ran back outside and there was Milo in his suit. He looked so handsome. For a dog, that is.

We walked down the driveway and up the street. "What is it like in court?" I asked. "What kind of dog is the judge?"

"Judges are usually Saint Bernards," Milo said. "Saint Bernards are the best judges because they are big and intimidating but they are also kind and gentle at the same time. Bull Dogs, on the other hand, don't take any guff at all, so they make great court marshals."

"Do you allow cats in the court room? Do they need their own cat lawyers?" I asked.

"Yes we do allow cats in the court room, they have rights too. Most of the time when cats are in court they are suing dogs for chasing them, but they never win," Milo said. "There are very few cats who are lawyers, mostly because they can't pass the bar exam. They get distracted too easily."

We walked into the park and up to a big tree. Milo pulled on a branch and a secret door opened. Inside was an elevator. We walked inside and the door closed. Milo pushed a button and the elevator started to move down. I was so excited, I couldn't stop smiling at Milo.

When the door opened I looked out and there were dogs everywhere. All different kinds of dogs, I couldn't believe my eyes. We left the elevator and walked past a group of dogs in paw cuffs and orange jump suits. "These dogs are on their way to jail for chasing cars. It is against the law to chase cars," Milo told me.

When we entered the court room, I was surprised to see dogs everywhere.
Almost all the seats were full, there were so many of them. Milo went to the
front of the room and sat at his table. Sitting next to Milo was a serious
looking Gray Hound. Milo told me his name was Chaser.

I watched as Milo presented his case to the judge. The judge was a Saint Bernard named Boris Olsen Nedward Egbert Smith, but all the dogs called him Judge Bones for short.

Milo was so great! I'm sure that's why he is the lawyer on this case, it was amazing to watch.

The lawyer for Balmart was a weasel named Slick Sam. Slick got up after Milo and argued his side of the case.

I didn't think he could be trusted. After Slick was done, the judge made us take a break so he could go into another room and decide the winner.

Judge
Bones

While the judge was in his room, I went to Milo and told him how proud I was of him. I said, "I think you're great for standing up for the rights of others."

He gave me a lick on my face and said "thanks." Then he asked, "how do you think I did?"

"You did great! If I were the judge I'd make you the winner for sure!"

Just then the judge came back and asked everyone to sit down. Judge Bones told the court how disappointed he was that he had to waste his time on such a terrible case.

The judge said that Milo had won the case and that Balmart would be fined 100,000 doggy treats.

All the dogs in the room were so excited Milo had won that they began to bark and howl. I couldn't believe it, my dog the lawyer had just won a huge case and I was there to see it! I ran to Milo, picked him up, and squeezed him.

He licked my face and said, "let's go home."

"Sounds great I can't wait to tell Mom and Dad about your big case!"

When we got home Milo went to the back yard, and I went into the kitchen. I heard my mom saying, "Milo does nothing but sleep all day."

"Well he is getting a little older, and that's what happens as dog's age," Dad replied.

I was about to tell my mom and dad that Milo isn't old he is amazing! But just then, Milo walked into the kitchen on all four legs. He had taken off his suit and tie.

Milo looked at me and winked. Then he walked over to my mom and started to beg for food. My mom grabbed a dog treat, kneeled down and scratched behind Milo's ear as she said, "you're not getting too old are you boy."

Milo just looked at her and begged for another treat. I opened my mouth to tell my mom how wrong she was when Milo looked at me, shook his head, and winked again.

I knew then that Milo's job would be our little secret. I have the greatest dog in the world and I love sharing this secret with him.

Made in the USA
Charleston, SC
20 August 2016